3

That day, Kangaroo and her joey
were playing near a stream.
Suddenly, they saw the old wombat.

"Can I help you?" asked Kangaroo.
"I'm hungry and thirsty,"
said the wombat. "I need some
water to drink and some grass
to eat."

"Hold on to my tail," said Kangaroo.
Kangaroo led the old wombat
to the stream to drink. Then she
led him to sweet grass to eat.
The old wombat was happy.

But when Kangaroo looked up,
her joey was gone. She looked
all around. Where was he?

HOW KANGAROO GOT HER POUCH

by Jackie Walter and Liza Murphy

FRANKLIN WATTS
LONDON•SYDNEY

Long ago, the god Byamee wanted to know who was the kindest animal. He came down to Earth as an old wombat to find out.

Then she saw him asleep under
a gum tree. Kangaroo left her joey
to sleep and went back to help
the wombat.

Then Kangaroo saw a hunter.
He was creeping towards
the wombat. She didn't know what
to do. She had to protect her joey.

Thump! Thump! Thump!

Kangaroo hit the ground with

her strong tail.

The hunter turned and saw her.

Kangaroo ran off into the bush,
and the hunter followed.
She led him away from the wombat
and away from her joey.

She ran and ran, deeper into
the bush. At last, she hid in a cave.
The hunter went by.
Kangaroo was safe.

Kangaroo went back to find her joey and the wombat. Her joey was still fast asleep under the gum tree. But the wombat was gone.

14

The old wombat turned back into the god Byamee. The god was pleased with how kind Kangaroo was.

Byamee made a bag from leaves.
He tied it around Kangaroo's waist.
"This is a pouch. You can put
your joey in it to keep him safe,"
he told her.

The bag grew soft fur. It became part of her body. Kangaroo was very happy with her gift. And now all kangaroos have a pouch to keep their joeys safe.

Story order

Look at these 5 pictures and captions.
Put the pictures in the right order
to retell the story.

1

Kangaroo finds her Joey asleep.

2

The god Byamee turns into a wombat.

20

3

Kangaroo gets a pouch.

4

Kanagroo helps the wombat.

5

Kangaroo sees the hunter.

Independent Reading

This series is designed to provide an opportunity for your child to read on their own. These notes are written for you to help your child choose a book and to read it independently.

In school, your child's teacher will often be using reading books which have been banded to support the process of learning to read. Use the book band colour your child is reading in school to help you make a good choice. *How Kangaroo Got her Pouch* is a good choice for children reading at Orange Band in their classroom to read independently. The aim of independent reading is to read this book with ease, so that your child enjoys the story and relates it to their own experiences.

About the book

Kangaroo is always losing her baby Joey. When an old wombat appears and sees how kind Kangaroo is, the wombat reveals it is really a god called Byamee. Kangaroo's kindness is rewarded and she is given a pouch to keep her joey in.

Before reading

Help your child to learn how to make good choices by asking: "Why did you choose this book? Why do you think you will enjoy it?" Look at the cover together and ask: "What do you think the story will be about?" Ask your child to think of what they already know about the story context. Then ask your child to read the title aloud. Establish that in this book they will learn about a Kangaroo and that a baby Kangaroo is called a joey. Ask: "What do you know about Kangaroos? Where do they live?"

Remind your child that they can sound out the letters to make a word if they get stuck.

Decide together whether your child will read the story independently or read it aloud to you.

During reading

Remind your child of what they know and what they can do independently. If reading aloud, support your child if they hesitate or ask for help by telling the word. If reading to themselves, remind your child that they can come and ask for your help if stuck.

After reading

Support comprehension by asking your child to tell you about the story. Use the story order puzzle to encourage your child to retell the story in the right sequence, in their own words. The correct sequence can be found at the bottom of the next page.

Help your child think about the messages in the book that go beyond the story and ask: "How did the god Byamee decide who was the kindest animal?"

Give your child a chance to respond to the story: "Did you have a favourite part? Did you think Kangaroo would find her joey? Why/why not?"

Extending learning

Help your child understand the story structure by using the same sentence patterning and adding different elements. "Let's make up a new story about another animal. Which animal is your story about? What could be special about that animal? How might it have got the part that makes it special, for example a rabbit and its ears?"

In the classroom, your child's teacher may be teaching about punctuation, such as the use of exclamation marks. There are examples in this book that you could look at with your child, for example: *Thump! Thump! Thump!* Find these together and point out how the apostrophe indicates emphasis or surprise.

Franklin Watts
First published in Great Britain in 2022
by Hodder and Stoughton

Copyright © Hodder and Stoughton Ltd, 2022

Series Editors: Jackie Hamley and Melanie Palmer
Development Editors and Series Advisors: Dr Sue Bodman and Glen Franklin
Series Designers: Peter Scoulding and Cathryn Gilbert

A CIP catalogue record for this book is
available from the British Library.

ISBN 978 1 4451 8388 6 (hbk)
ISBN 978 1 4451 8389 3 (pbk)
ISBN 978 1 4451 8449 4 (ebook)
ISBN 978 1 4451 8450 0 (library ebook)

Printed in China

Franklin Watts
An imprint of
Hachette Children's Group
Part of Hodder and Stoughton
Carmelite House
50 Victoria Embankment
London EC4Y 0DZ

An Hachette UK Company
www.hachette.co.uk

www.reading-champion.co.uk

Answer to Story order: 2, 4, 5, 1, 3